**DATE DUE**

11                                    c.1

KITCHEN, BERT

AUTHOR

SOMEWHERE TODAY

TITLE

| DATE LOANED | BORROWER'S NAME | DATE RETURNED |
|---|---|---|

11                                    c.1
Class                                Acc.


KITCHEN, BERT
(Author's Name)


SOMEWHERE TODAY
(Book Title)


OUR SAVIOR LUTHERAN CHURCH
(Library Ownership)

*For Sebastian Walker*

Copyright © 1992 by Bert Kitchen

First U.S. edition 1992
First published in Great Britain
in 1992 by Walker Books Ltd., London.

*Library of Congress Cataloging-in-Publication Data:*

Kitchen, Bert.
Somewhere today / by Bert Kitchen.
—1st U.S. ed.
Summary: Describes unusual animal rituals
of work, play, courtship, and survival.
1. Animal behavior—Juvenile literature.
[1. Animals—Habits and behavior.] I. Title.
QL751.5.K47  1992    91-58754   591.51—dc20
ISBN 1-56402-074-6

10 9 8 7 6 5 4 3 2

Printed and bound in Hong Kong by
Dai Nippon Printing Co. (H.K.) Ltd.

The pictures for this book were
done with acrylic paints.

Candlewick Press
2067 Massachusetts Avenue
Cambridge, Massachusetts 02140

# SOMEWHERE TODAY

## BY BERT KITCHEN

CANDLEWICK PRESS
CAMBRIDGE, MASSACHUSETTS

# Somewhere today a sea otter is floating on its back for lunch.

The sea otter is found along parts of the Pacific coast—and around its offshore islands—from the Bering Sea to California. Though it rarely ventures into water more than sixty-five feet deep, it does live almost exclusively at sea, mooring itself to a convenient bed of seaweed to sleep, and floating on its back to eat. It can even drink seawater.

The sea otter feeds on clams, sea urchins, mussels, abalones, and other mollusks, breaking their shells against a rock that it carries on its chest. It needs to eat about twenty pounds of shellfish meat—one-quarter of its own weight—every day. Unlike other marine animals, sea otters don't have insulating layers of fat. Pockets of air held within their dense fur enable them to float and keep warm.

# Somewhere today a pair of western grebes is running over water.

The western grebe of North America has short wings and almost no tail at all. Unlike most water birds, which have webbed feet, the grebe has stiff, horny fringes on each of its three front toes. These large-lobed toes work as paddles on or below the surface of the water.

When two grebes are courting, they perform a series of elaborate water displays. These include the "mating run," shown here, when male and female rise up and rush over the surface of the water.

# Somewhere today
# a chameleon
# is reaching out for food.

The Jackson's chameleon lives in East Africa—from Uganda and Tanzania up to northern Mozambique.

The chameleon is famous for its ability to change color, often merging with its surroundings. Less well known is the fact that it can shoot out its coiled-up tongue to the full length of its body. This makes it a formidable insect catcher.

The chameleon has superb eyesight and can move its eyes independently to look in two directions at once. When it has spotted a likely-looking insect, it takes aim with devastating accuracy. Its tongue, which has a sticky pad on the end of it, shoots out, picks up the insect, and recoils—all in a split second.

# Somewhere today
# an archerfish is taking aim.

The archerfish lives in India, Australia, and the Philippines.
It prefers the brackish waters around mangroves, but is also found
in the sea and in fresh water.
The archerfish cruises along just below the surface of the water, looking for
insects on the leaves or stems of overhanging vegetation. When it finds an insect,
it squirts drops of water at it to shoot it down.
Adult archerfish can aim accurately up to a distance of ten feet.

# Somewhere today
# two bald eagles, talons locked,
# are plummeting through the sky.

The bald eagle of North America, symbol of the United States, is an enormous bird, up to three feet long from head to tail. Its powerful outstretched wings can measure as much as eight feet across. It isn't really bald at all, but owes its name to the dramatic hood of white feathers on its head and neck, which gives it a bare-headed look from a distance.

Each year, the bald eagle returns to the same mate, renewing its courtship with a spectacular display of aerial acrobatics. Two eagles lock talons and fall through the sky, tumbling and somersaulting. Seconds before reaching the ground, they separate and soar up high again.

# Somewhere today
# two brown hares are boxing.

The common brown hare is found throughout Europe and Africa, in open country, farmland, and woods.

The hare can run amazingly fast—forty-five miles an hour at full gallop—but its sporting activities are not limited to running. When a female hare is being courted by a male, she often boxes with him.

# Somewhere today
# a spotted skunk
# is doing a handstand.

The western spotted skunk lives in an area extending from the western United States to central Mexico. When faced with a dangerous enemy, the skunk will throw itself onto its front paws, stretch itself up to its full height, and display the distinctive black-and-white markings on its back. This is a threat; a warning of what is to follow. If it fails to deter the potential attacker, the skunk will turn around, still upside-down, and direct a well-aimed, foul-smelling spray at it from special glands under its tail.

# Somewhere today
# two spectacled salamanders
# are striking a pose.

The spectacled salamander, which lives in western Italy, is usually at home on well-wooded mountainsides, close to clear streams. For the most part, it lives a nocturnal life, but it occasionally emerges in the early evening, or during the day if it has rained.

It is the only European salamander to have four toes on each foot. When threatened, the spectacled salamander exposes its brilliantly colored belly to deter its enemy. To do this, it might curl up its tail or, much more dramatically, fall on its back with its feet in the air, playing dead.

# Somewhere today
# two dung beetles are rolling
# a ball across the sand.

The South African dung beetle is related to the sacred scarab of Egypt and the Mediterranean countries.

Dung beetles work in pairs. They collect animal dung, shape it into a ball, and roll it to a place where the soil is suitable for its burial. Dung is food to the dung beetle. The female beetle lays her eggs on the dung ball so that her larvae have something to eat as soon as they emerge.

# Somewhere today a sidewinding rattlesnake is making tracks.

The sidewinder is found in the deserts of the southwestern United States—Nevada, Utah, California, and Arizona—and also northern Baja California in Mexico.

A sidewinder doesn't travel forward in a straight line, as other snakes do. It moves by throwing its head forward in the direction it wants to go, but keeping its body sideways: The body loops and flicks forward in response to the head movements. One advantage of this way of traveling is that only part of the snake is touching the hot sand at any one time.

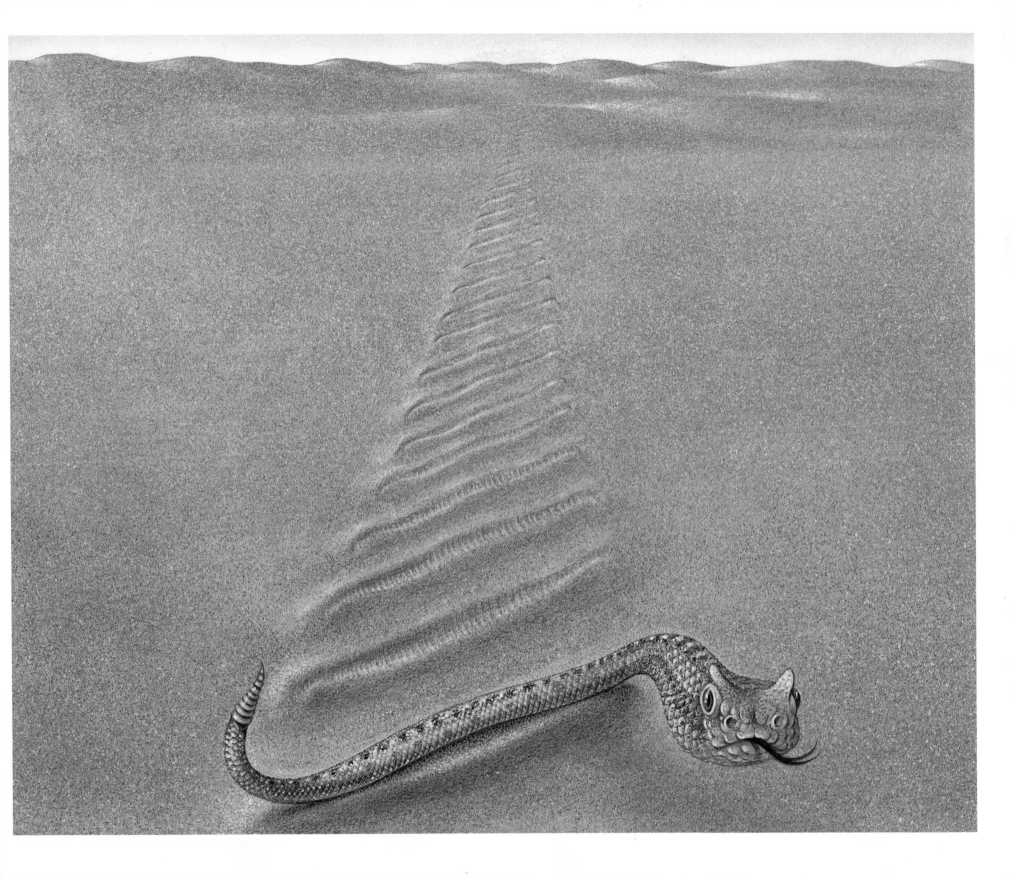

# Somewhere today
# a blue bird of paradise
# is hanging upside-down.

Prince Rudolph's blue bird of paradise inhabits the rainforests
in the mountains of southeastern New Guinea. When he wants to attract
a mate, the male bird gives a series of buglelike cries. Then he hangs
upside-down from a special courting branch with his brilliant plumage
spread out and his tail straps held in graceful curves. He swings to
and fro and utters a peculiar grating call.
Altogether irresistible.

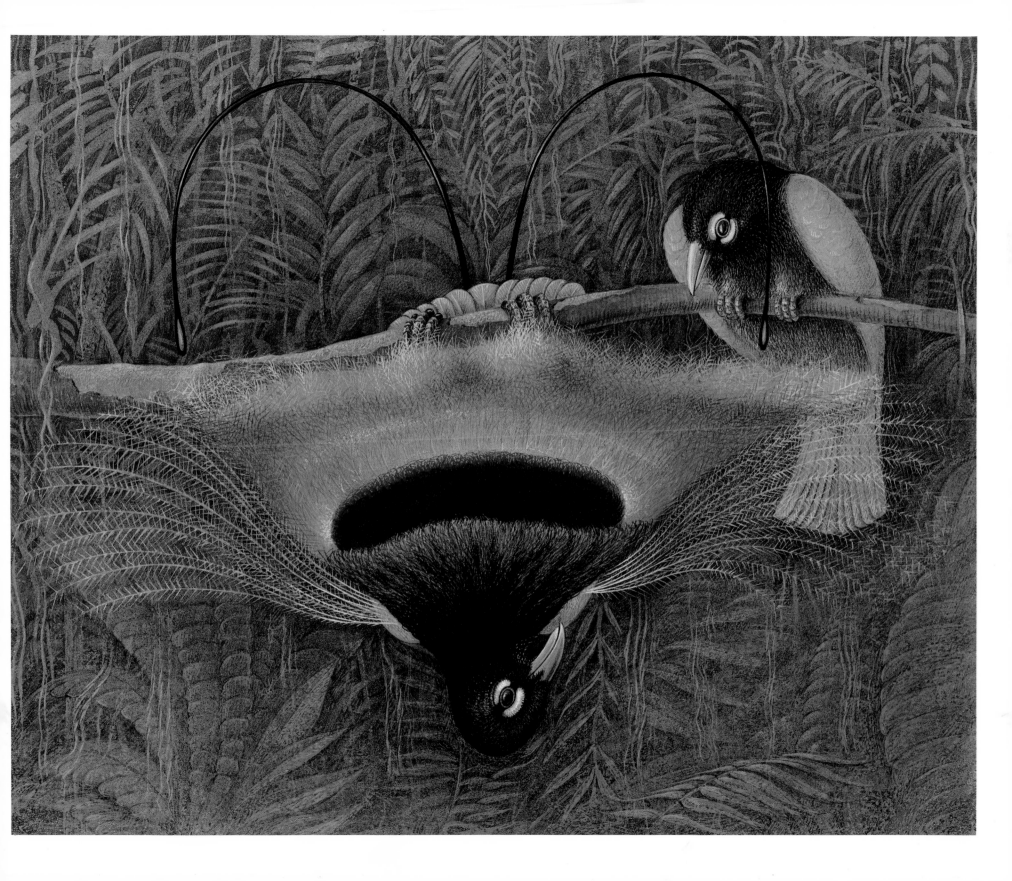

# And somewhere today a dormouse is sleeping.

The common or hazel dormouse is widespread in the forests and gardens of Europe. This tiny creature eats as much as it can during the summer, building up fat that it can live on during the cold season. At the beginning of winter, it builds itself a leaf and grass nest under fallen leaves, between tree stumps, or in a pile of wood. Then it curls itself up into a ball, wraps its bushy tail over its body, and settles down to sleep... for as long as nine months at a time.

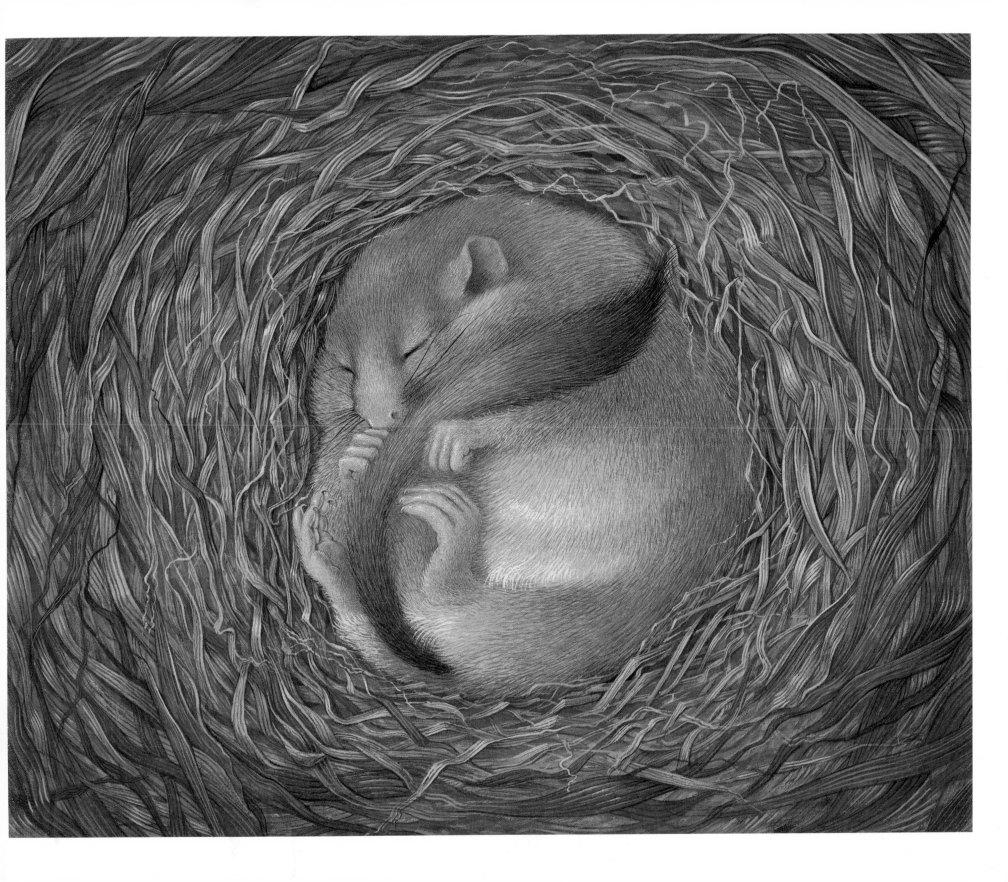